Pocket Pirates

The Great Treasure Hunt

4

Chris Mould

ALADDIN
New York London Toronto Sydney New Delhi

This book is a work of fiction. Any references to historical events, real people, or real places are used fictitiously. Other names, characters, places, and events are products of the author's imagination, and any resemblance to actual events or places or persons, living or dead, is entirely coincidental.

ALADDIN
An imprint of Simon & Schuster Children's Publishing Division
1230 Avenue of the Americas, New York, New York 10020
This Aladdin paperback edition September 2019

Originally published in Great Britain by Hodder Children's Books
Published under license from the British publisher
Hodder & Stoughton Limited on behalf of its publishing imprint
Hodder Children's Books, a division of Hachette Children's Group
Also available in an Aladdin hardcover edition.

Cover designed by Tiara Iandiorio
Interior designed by Mike Rosamilia
The illustrations for this book were rendered in pen and ink.
The text of this book was set in New Century Schoolbook.
Manufactured in the United States of America 0819 OFF
2 4 6 8 10 9 7 5 3 1
Library of Congress Control Number 2019930887
ISBN 978-1-4814-9124-2 (hc)
ISBN 978-1-4814-9123-5 (pbk)
ISBN 978-1-4814-9125-9 (eBook)

FOR
THE STAFF
AND
CHILDREN
OF
LONG
DITTON
ST. MARY'S
JUNIOR SCHOOL

BUTTON
LILY
THE BASEBOARD MICE

CAPTAIN CRABSTICKS
OLD UNCLE NOGGIN
JONES
MR. DREGBY

CONTENTS

The Old
Junk Shop

At the end of the street is an old junk shop. It's gloomy and shabby and nothing ever happens there. At least, that's what most people think. . . .

Among the odds and ends and things of no use, a dusty ship in a bottle sits gathering cobwebs on a shelf. But when the world isn't watching, a tiny pirate crew comes out to explore.

And when you're smaller than a teacup, a junk shop can be a pretty dangerous place. . . .

The Cheese Joke

A black beetle clung tightly to the back of Button the cabin boy. Button gasped and puffed as its hook-like feet buried themselves into his sides and shoulders. His hands gripped the shoelace hard, but he made the mistake of looking down and felt sick. It was a long way.

"Just a bit further," he grunted.

Finally he grasped the edge of the shelf and pulled himself up with all his might, his arms burning. He lay flat, breathing heavily.

After a moment he got to his knees and pulled the beetle from his shoulder. It scurried off into a corner, receiving a warm welcome from its family. They darted around Button's legs, clicking excitedly.

"There you go," he said. "Make sure you don't let your little ones wander too near the edge next time." And the beetles scampered off, click-click-clicking their thanks.

"Ah, you're such a good friend to the animals, Button. Well done." It was Button's shipmate Lily, back from a morning stroll.

"Poor little chap," said Button. "He'd fallen all the way down into the book box. It's a good thing he has that shell on his back. And those mice would have made a good supper of him."

Further along the shelf Captain Crabsticks, head pirate of the pocket-sized crew, had spotted a new book. "There's

not much gets past the old Captain," he muttered to himself. Though it must be admitted that the book was the size that a small castle would be to you and me, so it wasn't too impressive that the Captain had noticed it.

He ran his hand along the spine and tipped his head sideways to read it. *"Secret Treasures of the Ancient World."*

For the rest of the morning the Captain was lost inside the book. He enjoyed it so much that lunch wandered by unnoticed. He was, in fact, missing out on a rather large portion of hard-boiled egg.

"Where is the Captain?" mumbled Button, filling his face.

"Tried calling him," said Lily. "No answer."

Jones the ship's cat meowed under the jam-jar-lid tabletop and Button fed him a scrap.

"Well, all the more for us then," said

Old Uncle Noggin, who wasn't going to miss the chance of an extra slice.

"Hmmmmmm, fascinating," said the Captain to himself as he started to make his way back toward the old ship in the bottle.

He screwed up his face and scratched his chin. "I've discovered a very *serious* problem," he continued. "I'm going to have to rally round the rest of the miniature pirate crew. Our position as rulers of the old junk shop shelves is at great risk. The buccaneers need to know why, and the sooner the better so that we can get this sorted. Now where is that work-shy lot, I wonder?"

By now, Button was sneaking an afternoon nap in the bottom of a broken egg cup at the back of the shelf. The soles of his shoes pointed up at the ship in the bottle as it towered proudly above him.

Inside, the rest of the crew were busy at their work. Well when I say "busy at their work," I mean Old Uncle Noggin was starting to eat his way through a clump of sticky marshmallow he'd found, while Lily was lying in her hammock mending holes in her socks. She was using stolen strands of silky spider thread, pinched from Mr. Dregby's web. The house spider would not be pleased if he found out!

Button woke with a start when the

Captain sounded the ship's horn. Lily almost fell out of her hammock: it was her turn to climb the mast and blow into the snail shell to announce dinner. This was a duty that only fell to her or Button: Old Uncle Noggin was too chubby to climb the mast, and of course the Captain was too important.

Button looked up at the face of the wristwatch hanging on the wall. It was five o'clock already. And there was the Captain climbing down from sounding the ship's horn. What could be important enough to get him to scale the mast?

In a moment, the crew were ready. They were never happier than when poised for a pirate dinner. But Captain Crabsticks was making an announcement.

"Now listen here, my fellow buccaneers. We have a major problem. Something is MISSING."

"WHAT?" asked Old Uncle Noggin, keen to get to his dinner.

"Well, what do you think?" continued the Captain. "Tell me, what do we have on board our ship?"

"We've got everything we need," said Button. "There's food, there's a good water supply from the leaky pipe. We've got blankets made out of that pair of giant purple underpants, our mustard-pot bathtub, and we've even got fresh fruit!"

"It's a rotten apple core," pointed out Lily.

"Errm, true," butted in Old Uncle Noggin, "but we've got a quarter of a custard cream, a whole thimbleful of sugar, *and* three types of cheese."

The conversation wasn't going the way the Captain had wanted.

"Never mind all that. I wasn't talking about our shopping list!"

"*Three* types of cheese? I didn't think we had three. Name them!" insisted Button to Old Uncle Noggin.

The Captain gave up trying to make his point. He stood, hands on hips, and waited patiently for his rowdy crew.

"Well, there's a whole slice of Cheddar, a bag of crumbly bits of Wensleydale and cranberry, and the other one begins with a G but I can never remember the name of it. . . ."

"Gruyère?" suggested Button.

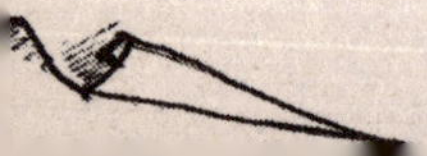

"No."

"Goat's cheese?" said Lily.

"No."

"It must be Gorgonzola," snapped the Captain.

"No, it's none of those."

"Well I can't think of anything else," said Lily.

"Ah, I remember," announced Old Uncle Noggin with a smile. "It's *grated*."

"Right, if you've quite finished talking about cheese," said the Captain, "I need to make my point and it's a jolly good one. Pin back those lugs and get listening."

"Aye, aye, Cap'n, do tell us, what IS

missing from our galleon?" asked Old Uncle Noggin.

"Well, I've been doing a spot of reading about pirate life and it appears we're without something VERY obvious."

"WHATTTT?" said Button, raising his hands in the air.

"Pirate gold!" said the Captain. "We don't have a single nugget of pure pirate gold! How can we call ourselves pirates if

all we've got is moldy cheese and rotten fruit?"

"And what do you suppose we do about that?" asked Button.

"I'll tell you what we need to do about it, young sea urchin. We need to empty out all our rubbish from that great big trunk and fill it with precious booty, otherwise we're never going to be taken seriously as pirates."

"And where do you think it is, this *pirate gold*?" asked Lily.

"Well, there must be some somewhere, old chap. This place is filled with wonders and curiosities. Endless piles of undiscovered delights. We're not proper pirates if we can't find buried treasure here."

Lily *hated* it when he called her "old chap," but it was a habit and the Captain wasn't going to change. She ignored it and carried on.

"It's true that everybody loves a good gold hunt, don't they?"

Button gave Lily a wide grin. "Yes, they do," he said. "Of course they do."

Their pirate dinner was a celebration that night. A sliver of ham, four bread crumbs, a chunk of the yellow bit from a boiled egg, and even a dollop of caramel from a chocolate.

When he couldn't eat any more, Button wandered off on his own. There was noth-

ing he liked more than sitting on the edge of the shelf, watching the sun go down. He fed bits of splintered wood and tiny chunks of apple to his friends the beetles until it got dark, then strolled back and perched inside his egg cup. Leaning over the edge with his arms folded he peered out over the shop, dreaming of long-lost treasure.

In the morning, they would start their hunt.

Into the Toy Box

Uncle Noggin announced he was going to stay and keep guard over the cheese. Supplies were especially good at the moment, and they didn't want to risk losing them to the baseboard mice if they all went venturing out together.

"I'll stay here and keep an eye on

the old sea dog," said Captain Crabsticks. He winked. "You young ones can go and do the looting. See what you can find. Holler if you need me, old chaps. I'm right here."

Button and Lily wore huge grins. Much as they loved Uncle Noggin, he slowed them down and it was always more fun to go it alone.

"A quick story before yer go, young hearties," said Old Uncle Noggin. "To set you on your way and get your minds thinking."

"Oh . . . er, go on then," said Button, hoisting his bag over his shoulder. "What is it about?"

"It's about searching, Button. About seeking and finding. It's a good lesson, that's what it is."

Button perched on the edge of a cotton reel, and Lily crossed her legs on the floor.

"Once, there was an astronomer who used to spend his days asleep and all his nights outside observing the stars."

"Er, what's an astronomer?" asked Button.

"Oh, here we go," said Lily. "Interruptions already."

Old Uncle Noggin patiently explained that an astronomer was a person who studied the sky and stars, then he carried on.

“One evening, as he wandered through the nighttime city with all his thoughts fixed on the sky above him, he fell into a deep well. He lay there in pain for some time, holding on tight to his bruises and crying out for help. Eventually a neighbor heard him and ran to the well. He peered in and through the dark he could just make out the man at the bottom. ‘What happened to you?’ said the neighbor. When the astronomer had described his fall, the neighbor asked him, ‘Old fellow, why, while trying to see what is up in heaven, do you not manage to see what is on earth?’”

“Is that it?” asked Button.

"Yes, that is it," tutted Old Uncle Noggin.

"Well, it's not much of a story," Button replied.

"Well, just maybe it's one of those stories that has a meaning you have to think about. Maybe it will mean something to you when you go treasure-hunting," said Uncle Noggin, tapping his nose and winking.

Lily was tapping her foot. "Er, are we ready?"

"Yup, let's go!" said Button. "Thanks, Uncle Noggin. REALLY helpful." He rolled his eyes at Lily. "And well worth the wait."

Button adored the old pirate, but

sometimes his stories left him a little cold. Perhaps it would make sense when he'd thought about it a little longer!

In no time at all Button and Lily were scaling down the huge encyclopedias and clambering over odds and ends toward an unexplored corner of the junk shop. A new batch of clutter was there that they hadn't yet investigated.

They took a shortcut through a hole chewed in the corner of a box of teacups and teapots. When they came out on the other side they felt like they were in another world.

They were surrounded by toys. Dozens of tin robots, dolls, faces looming at them. They looked up in wonder. A wooden dragon on wheels with orange eyes.

"How come we've never seen all this before?" asked Button.

"Maybe it's new?" said Lily.

"There MUST be treasure here," insisted Button.

"Why?"

"Dunno," said Button. "It just seems . . . magical. Like there's something here. Maybe the robots are guarding something."

"Huh? And you say Uncle Noggin talks nonsense. Dear oh dear!" She grinned.

Just then Lily was startled by a shuffling noise. A scratching and scrabbling.

"What was that?" hissed Lily.

"What was WHAT?" replied Button.

“That noise.”

“What noise?”

“Hmmm. Nothing. It’s probably just me.”

Button was too busy examining a tin model of a space rocket to take much notice.

They climbed into the top of the rocket and took a long look out across the toys. A sea of heads and hair, wood and metal, puppets and robots. And a nose, a long pink nose and sharp eyes.

Then the nose moved and there was a shuffling noise, the whip of a tail and a high-pitched squeak.

“I told you I heard something,” said Lily. “MICE.”

Button felt his heart thump into action. He could see three of them now, matted brown fur against the fading reds and yellows of the toys, sniffing the air. Fleabag, Blue Vinny, and Pepper Jack.

Vinny sharpened his claws against the rusted edge of a tin duck, like nails down a chalkboard.

"What do we do now?" gasped Lily.

"We do this . . . ," said Button. He climbed from the rocket onto a tall tin robot, grabbed the key in its back, and wound it tighter and tighter with all his strength.

"Here," said Lily, "let me help."

Together they wound the robot until the key wouldn't make another turn. Then they leaped across to the next one, watching out for the spiky fur and claws of the baseboard mice.

It wasn't easy to turn the keys on

the robots: they were huge and rusty, but Button and Lily were strong and fast. They wound up the next and the next, until their hands hurt and the box had a great tin army on the march. The force of the stomping metal feet weakened the cardboard edges of the box, making them pop open and letting the robots spill out on the floor. Some fell on their sides with their feet still working away; the others kept going, sending teacups and books toppling over.

The rag-tailed mouse varmints had no choice but to flee. Lily and Button perched on top of the rocket, watching the mice scatter in panic to all corners of the shop.

But the Pocket Pirates knew that those miserable mice would be back in a flash. Treasure-hunting in the open wilderness of the shop was too dangerous: they needed to hide, and quickly.

A Beautiful Home

Button and Lily had no time to enjoy the view. They could see the perfect place for escape: an old dolls' house was up ahead.

They couldn't be sure if they were imagining it or not, but as they clambered down from the rocket they thought they could hear the scratch and scrabble of mice, close behind them. They tore toward the house at lightning speed. Lily threw a glance behind her. “Faster!” she shouted. “They’re here!”

Button knew exactly where he was heading. He ignored the front door and hurled himself instead through a tiny half-open window, letting out an "OOMPH!" as Lily crash-landed on top of him.

The mice poked their huge sniffing noses through the window, but it was too small for them to get inside. They snarled and muttered through the gap, then disappeared with their tails whipping up behind them.

Button knew that now they'd been spotted out and about it would not be easy to escape from the mice. They would find a way inside. Lily raced to the front door and blocked it shut with an old roll of parcel tape, as Button watched the mouse crew disappear around the back of the house.

"This treasure-hunting is dangerous pirate business," said Button. He couldn't see the mice, but he could still hear them. "You know what I always say, Lil!"

"What's that, Button?"

"We'd be much safer out to sea on that ship. Dry land is not for the faint-hearted."

He pushed the little window closed, and it was only when he stood back that he realized the dolls' house was sitting at an angle. His whole body was sliding backward, and he had to hold on to a

doorway to stop himself tumbling into the next room.

With Lily at his side he began to venture through the house, pulling at the furniture and walls to help move onward. Every now and then they'd lose their grip and go sliding back down the slope.

"One step forward, two steps back!" said Button. "We'll get there eventually."

"Where are we heading, though?" asked Lily.

"I'm not exactly sure," admitted Button, and they both started shaking with laughter.

"We have to keep quiet!" giggled Lily.

"I've got an idea," said Button, forcing himself to stop laughing. He took the trusty shoelace from his backpack and lassoed it around a banister at the top of the stairs.

"Grab my waist," he instructed.

With Lily behind him, he mountaineered his way up the house.

"There's EVERYTHING we need in here, Lil," gasped Button as they passed through the kitchen. "Tables, chairs. Teapots, cups, and saucers. Plates and pans and pots!"

"Most of it is no use," Lily pointed out.

"Why?"

"We can't cook in pans made of plastic!"

"But some of it is all right," Button insisted, pointing at a beautiful clock with a long case. "You see? Look at this. A proper working clock."

It was handmade, intricately carved and painted. They listened for ticking. "Nothing," said Lily. "It doesn't work."

"It just needs winding," said Button. "Look, there's a little crank."

"Button, haven't we got better things to do than mess around with a grandfather clock? We're supposed to be treasure-seeking. That means gold!"

Just then a frantic scratching came from below, and they caught sight of a large claw hooked onto the staircase, a pink nose, and sharp eyes.

"They're here!" cried Lily.

Hearts racing, they pulled themselves up the stairs, trying to ignore the horrible scrabbling sounds as the mice tried to climb after them. Panicking, Button shoved the clock with his feet as he passed, letting it fall so that it halfblocked the stairs. They thundered through the door at the top

and barricaded themselves into a large bedroom.

"Look," said Lily, "an actual bed!" She threw herself onto it, but it was hard and she yelped in pain.

"Ha, not like the comforts of our hammocks, Lil!" laughed Button.

"Even the pillows are wooden," Lily groaned.

Button tugged at a door leading out of the bedroom.

"This way, Lil—there's a staircase into the attic. Maybe we can escape through the roof and leave those pesky mice behind for good."

The attic room looked like a study,

with a desk and a bookcase carved to look like there were endless volumes of encyclopedia filling the shelves. In the corner they could see the enormous catch where the front of the dolls' house could be opened up.

And then they noticed it. Indeed, how could they have missed it? A huge jewelry box shoved in the corner!

They stopped and stared. "I think we've struck gold!" cried Button.

Lily grinned. "Whoooaaaa. Here be treasure!"

It was a human-size jewelry box and they just knew it would be filled with pirate gold.

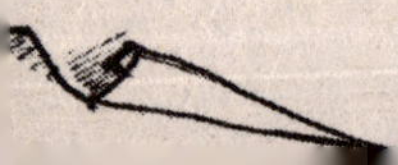

“Let’s double-check that door and make sure those rotten rodents definitely aren’t heading in here,” said Button. “We’ve got some pirate digging to do!”

The Girl in the Jewelry Box

They stood looking up at the jewelry box. It had a small clasp that, for Mr. Tooey, would just need a little press downward. But for the Pocket Pirates it was going to need a good thump with something hard.

Button dragged the chair from the

desk and climbed onto it. "Hold the back of the chair, Lil!"

"Please!" she said, glaring at him.

"SORRY. Please. Pretty please, with a cherry on the top."

"I should think so, young man."

"You're the young one," he said, smiling.

"I'm taller than you . . . and wiser!"

He climbed right up, standing on the back of the chair and hauling himself onto the lid of the box. Once he'd gotten his balance, he jumped onto the clasp with all his strength. As he tumbled off, he could hear the catch release.

Button fetched another chair. He and Lily stood on their chairs at two corners of the lid.

"I can feel my heart beating," said Lily.

"It's because we're real pirates, Lily, that's why. We're on a treasure hunt."

"It's like the moment when you're digging for gold and suddenly you can feel something in the sand."

"Like you've gotten ahold of the lid of a treasure chest!"

"Exactly," said Lily. "And you're about to look inside. . . ."

"PUSH!" yelled Button.

Together they prized the lid up and shoved it back. It creaked and wobbled

and for a moment it felt like it might come crashing back down.

But it didn't. As it opened a ballerina sprang upward and danced, turning slowly to the music suddenly coming from the box. She wore a leotard and a frilly lace skirt that appeared to be lifted by her pirouetting. Button and Lily were entranced.

Gradually she slowed and stopped. There was a mirror behind her and Button could see his own face, staring.

"What are you looking at, cabin boy?" said Lily, grinning.

"Nothing," said Button, realizing he'd been lost in a trance.

"It's a dummy, you dummy," she quipped.

“Oh . . . yeah, I know.” Button took his hands slowly off the lid, half expecting it to crash down on him. The box smelled old and a bit damp, like most of the things in the shop.

They climbed in, feeling the red velvet lining beneath their feet. Except for three or four wooden beads and a few hair clips, the box was empty. Not a trace of hidden treasure. Then they spotted a drawer at the back with a shiny handle.

"Let's try in there!" said Lily.

Button tugged at the drawer. It was stuck fast, with time and dust and damp, but he gave one final yank and it burst open.

Out streamed an army of earwigs, rearing up at them, scratching and grasping with their strange armored bodies.

Button drew the broken toothpick from his rucksack, his expression turning from *excited treasure-seeker's grin* to *fierce swordsman's determined glare.* Lily took off her hat and began to swipe at the earwigs, kicking the beads to send them rolling in all directions.

"There's nothing in the drawer, Button! No gold, just a filthy stinking insect den!" Lily cried in disappointment.

The tiny pirates found themselves hurdling

over their enemies, jumping this way and that until in the end all they could do was retreat out of the box and leap back into the attic room, leaving the ballerina girl to dance among the insects alone.

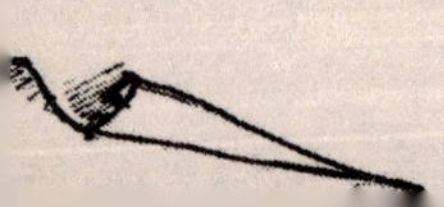

A Brush with Danger

They escaped, forcing open a window in the roof and clambering out onto the little wooden tiles.

"That was close," said Button, wiping his brow and feeling the scratches on his face.

"You and your adventures," said Lily,

leaning against the chimney stack. "I think I've had enough of them for a lifetime. I'd be much better off staying at home and relaxing in my hammock."

Button grinned.

"What are you smiling at, buccaneer boy?" Lily asked.

"It just feels good to have an adventure," laughed Button. "I know it gets scary sometimes . . . but it just feels right. We're pirates, Lil. It's what we do."

"Oh . . . oh really," Lily said, pointing out over the shop. Footsteps were echoing down the hallway.

Mr. Tooey appeared, armed with dusters and brushes and heading toward the Pocket Pirates' shelf. Button and Lily hid behind the chimney, peeking out to see what was happening.

"Trust him to turn up," muttered Lily. "What's he doing in the shop so early? It's not lunchtime yet, is it?"

Then their mouths dropped open in horror, and they stared wild-eyed as he picked up the ship in the bottle. He was springing a tidying session on the old junk-shop shelf!

And though Mr Tooey didn't notice, Old Uncle Noggin was hanging out of the bottle's opening and gripping on for dear life.

"Oh no!" screamed Lily, her small voice unheard across the shop. "Hang on, Uncle Noggin!" She held her hands to her mouth in horror, slipped, and started cascading down the tiles. Button grabbed her arm, pulled her back and held on tight.

Mr. Tooey walked across the tiles and placed the bottle gently on the floor, all without catching sight of Old Uncle Noggin.

"Disastrous!" said Button. "He needs to get back into the bottle NOW! If the mice get near, our buccaneering brother has had it. And right now, those mice are ANGRY!"

And then just as Old Uncle Noggin had almost pulled himself through the opening in the neck, they watched Mr. Tooey accidentally knock the bottle across the floor. It went rolling across the floor, the ship turning and turning. Uncle Noggin's tummy was wedged in the opening, his little old legs flying around like a spinning top. Whizzing in circles like he was on a waltzer and he wasn't going to stop until BANG, it crashed into the baseboard.

Old Uncle Noggin was thrown out and splattered against the wall.

Button and Lily were frozen with fear.

Lily imagined their captain going tumbling around the inside of the ship. Jones, the ship's cat, was probably not in a good state either. The whole place would

be a mess. Button thought of his room, everything upturned and out of place.

Mr. Tooey had chased the bottle and tried to stop it with his foot, but as he bent to inspect it Old Uncle Noggin was hidden by the ship. "Seems all right," muttered Mr. Tooey, leaving it be.

Button and Lily held their breath, hoping for a sign of their captain or for Old Uncle Noggin to pick himself up off the floor. Mr. Tooey ran his old brush along the shelf, whistling as if nothing had happened. Didn't he know that he had just caused a major disaster in the world of *small*? But he didn't seem to have noticed anything as he gathered odds and ends into a box.

"There goes our cotton reel," said Button.

"And your outdoor sleeping area," added Lily.

"Outdoor sleeping area?"

"The broken egg cup. You're always asleep inside the broken egg cup."

"I *once* fell asleep inside the broken egg cup."

And still there was no sign of the other Pocket Pirates.

The sound of the clock striking midday made Button and Lily jump. It always brought everything to a halt—no matter what Mr. Tooey was doing, it meant he would stop for lunch. Off he went, back to the place called Fridge.

"Quick," said Button. "Let's head over to the bottle."

They shinned down the roof, grabbing

onto the gutter, sliding clumsily down the little wooden drainpipe glued to the front of the dolls' house. It creaked and groaned and they felt it come away from the wall as they lowered themselves. They bashed onto the paving outside the house, tried to ignore the pain, and raced over to help Uncle Noggin. He was already trying to fight off the baseboard mice with the first thing that came to hand. This just happened to be a pink cocktail umbrella.

"Get back!" yelled Lily as she thrashed at them with a lump of sticky marshmallow. It was all she could find—but it worked. As the mice tried to fend

it off with their sharp teeth it stuck their mouths together, and they were forced to retreat to their hole.

Just then Captain Crabsticks appeared, looking like he'd been put through a laundry cycle. "Ahoy, young Button. Cast your rope aboard, my fine fellow! We have a rather untidy deck up here."

Button's shoelace had already bailed them out once today. He pulled it from his backpack and hurled it up for the Captain to secure.

They sent Uncle Noggin up first and prayed that the shoelace would hold, since it was already frayed and worn. Up

the old pirate went, slowly but surely.

"You next, Lil," said Button.

"Oh, you are a gentleman after all!" grinned Lily.

"Hurry up," said Button, climbing up after her.

He hadn't exactly expected a hero's welcome, but he was still a little surprised by Uncle Noggin's greeting.

"Err . . . you owe me some marsh-mallow, young Button." Old Uncle Noggin had his cross face on.

"But . . . I just helped save your life."

"Well, yes, technically speaking, you did. But you know what I'm like if I don't get my sugary snacks. I get all grumpy."

"Huh, well you almost became someone else's sugary snack just now, so think yourself lucky."

"Now, now, now, never mind sticky marshmallow nonsense," put in the Captain. "What on earth are we going to do with this ship? It's a complete wreck."

The mini pirates had waged war with mice and insects, battled with the biggest of spiders. But never before had they needed to repair a shipwrecked vessel. Every bit of its contents seemed to be broken. Only the ship itself seemed intact.

"Where on earth do we start?" asked the Captain.

"I'm not sure," said Button. "But

there's something else I'm worried about."

"What?" quizzed Lily.

"Where is Jones?"

But Jones was nowhere to be seen.

Seeking Jones

The whole ship was a disaster. The jam-jar-lid dinner table had been hurled across the ship and its matchbox base was dented and squashed. Anything that wasn't nailed down had been thrown around like laundry in a tumble dryer.

"Did *you* see Jones?" asked Button,

hoping the Captain would know where he was.

"Certainly not, old chap. Haven't seen him anywhere. I was too busy hanging on to my hat as I was thrown around the cabin like a rag doll."

"What if the mice got him, in the middle of the mayhem?" gasped Button.

"Oh . . . *no,*" said Lily, a tremble of fear in her voice. She rushed off into the ship, calling Jones's name.

"Look," said the Captain. "I say. The old clock has been ruined."

On the floor was the wristwatch face that had hung on the wall, shattered into a thousand pieces. Cogs and glass and tiny

hammers and little screws were laid out in front of them like an unsolvable puzzle.

“Oh, dear,” said Old Uncle Noggin. “It’s ruined for good.”

“What a mess. It looks like we’ve been robbed!” said the Captain.

“We’d never do this to anybody,” said Button. “We might be pirates, but we’re only Fridge raiders. We’ve got good hearts.”

“Don’t worry, lad,” said Old Uncle Noggin. “Old Mr. Tooey don’t know we’re here, does he? Ain’t his fault. He’s only keeping the old place tidy, and we’ll soon have our ship back to where it was.”

“But we don’t have our clock anymore, and we still don’t know where Jones is and

everything is broken," groaned Button.

He followed Lily into their cabin, just in case Jones had been hiding there all along. But she'd found nothing, and the room was smashed to pieces. His matchstick-box wardrobe had toppled over and been crushed, the hammocks were in twisted knots, and everything else they owned seemed to be either torn or broken. Lily sighed in defeat and went back to join the rest of the crew.

Then, in the silence, Button's hammock shuffled and rustled. The twisted lumps of cloth seemed to be moving.

Button drew closer.

And then . . . the hammock meowed.

"JONES," said Button calmly. "There

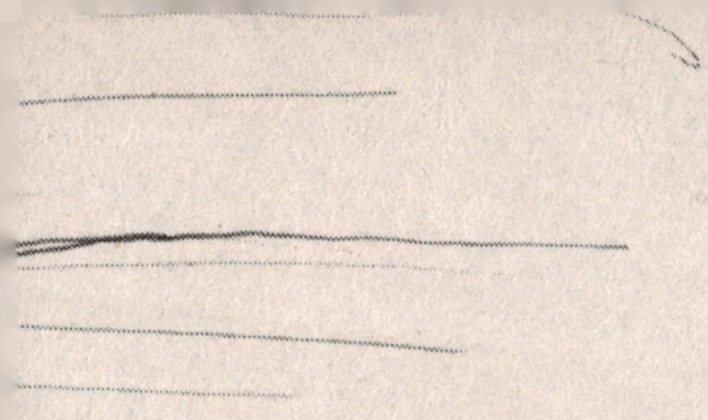

you are, old boy. I thought I'd never find you."

They sat on the hammock together and Button held the small cat tight.

"He's here!" cried Button. The rest of the crew rushed in, making a huge fuss of Jones. He purred noisily at every stroke of his fur and dug his head into Button's side as if he never wanted to let go of him again.

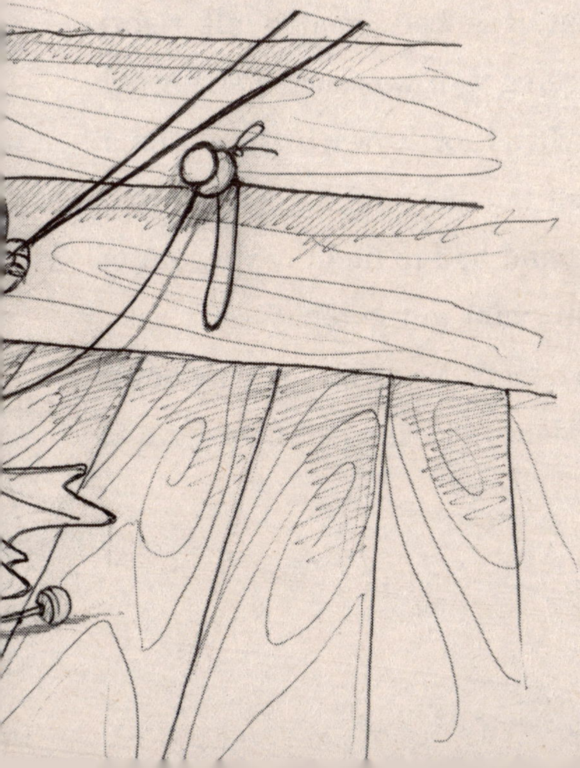

"Ah, bless his tail and whiskers. Poor old mog," said Old Uncle Noggin. "Reminds me of the time I got trapped in the bottom of an old sock."

"Oh, here we go," whispered Button to Lily. "Prepare yourself for another of Old Uncle Noggin's tales!"

"Terrible it was. Not the being trapped bit. No, that was bad enough all right, especially seeing as it was such a stripy old stinker. But then I got thrown in the washing machine! Felt the drum filling up with cold soapy water and had to find my way out of the sock and swim to the top. Wasn't easy, mind you. Thought I was on my way down to old Davy Jones's locker. But here I am to

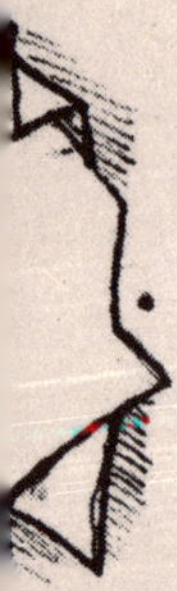

tell the tale. Didn't need a bath for a long time after that, I can promise you."

Lily and Button chuckled then fell silent. "What a disappointment today has been," said Button, sighing.

"What do you mean?" asked Lily.

"Well, we were set for a day of treasure-hunting, bug-bashing adventure. And in the end all we've got is a ship that looks like it's had cannonballs fired at it all night long."

Button stood stroking Jones in his arms, staring out of a porthole window.

"Come on," said Lily. "It's not been *that* bad. At least we're all OK."

"Yeah, for now," said Button, still looking out of the round window. "But Mr. Tooey will be back before long, and he's clumsy at the best of times."

"You're right," said Lily. "We'd better brace ourselves, hang on to our hats, and prepare for the worst. He'll be putting us back on the shelf soon."

"We need to do something to save the day, Lil," said Button.

"Like what?"

"I'm thinking," Button muttered. "I might just have an idea bubbling up."

Retrieving Old Father Time

"You've got that stupid look on your face again, Button," said Lily.

"What stupid look?"

"That look you have when you've got a crazy idea in your head and you've convinced yourself it will work. That look that worries me . . . A LOT!"

"I think we have to abandon our treasure hunt," suggested Button, looking toward the Captain for permission.

"Oh . . . well, I guess it's not a bad idea . . . for the time being," muttered the Captain. "The old place is ruined."

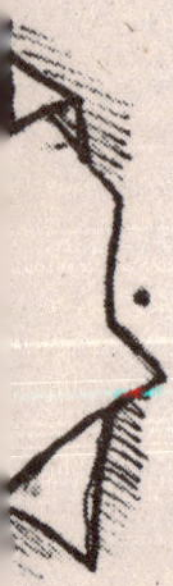

Button and Lily had never seen the Captain looking so broken. He was such a cheerful old soul that whenever he looked even vaguely miserable it felt like

the world had come to an end.

"Ah, shame about the treasure," said Old Uncle Noggin. "But at least the food supplies are OK." He rubbed his tummy. "I'll probably be a bit peckish soon. I haven't eaten for an hour or so."

Button grabbed Lily by the hand and hauled her off to check on the supplies. But it was not good news. The thimble jam pot had fallen into the butter and squashed the cheese underneath it. The biscuit bits had been crumbled so much that they'd turned from crumbs to dust and were falling between the floorboards of the ship. Most of the rest of the food seemed to have been shaken out of the bottle.

"I don't know where to start," said Lily, head in her hands.

"Look!" said Button. Lily joined him at the porthole and they watched as the sneaky mice scurried past with broken bits of the Pocket Pirates' food.

"Those cheeky . . ."

"Now now, old boy," said the Captain calmly. "They've gotten away with it this time. Don't let them get to you. We've a lot of tidying up to do."

"What's the point in starting before we get back on the shelf?" pointed out Lily. "We might as well wait until we're back in position, or we'll end up with the old place upside down again."

"Come on," Button whispered to Lily. "There's something important we need to do."

"I thought you'd abandoned the treasure hunt?" said Old Uncle Noggin.

"Yup. We have," Button replied as they headed off again.

"Don't leave me here to tidy all your mess! Garggggh, young 'uns. They're all the same!" cried Uncle Noggin.

"I say, old chaps, where are you bumbling off to?" grumbled the Captain.

"Be back soon!"

"Where ARE we going?" asked Lily.

"You'll see," said Button. "I have an idea about how to cheer up the Captain . . . and we have to do it before Mr. Tooey puts the bottle back on the shelf!"

They scampered off.

"Come on, Lil. Old Mr. Tooey will be back at exactly one o'clock. You know how strict he is about his lunch hour."

Lily was hot on Button's heels as he sprinted back toward the box of old toys.

They kept a keen eye out for the mice as they went.

In no time they were back in the old dolls' house, climbing the slope toward the staircase.

"Right," said Button. "What do you think?" He was standing next to the grandfather clock.

"About what?" asked Lily.

"About this," Button said, patting the clock.

"What about it?"

"It's a working clock, Lily. It's perfect. Ours is broken, and this doesn't belong here—it's too precious. It belongs on board our ship."

"But . . ."

“But what?”

“But . . . how would we even get it back? It’s huge.”

“Don’t worry about that just yet. Help me get it down the stairs.”

“But . . .”

“Here, get this corner,” said Button. “I’ll get the other side.”

And before Lily could even begin to protest that it was impossible, she was tugging and lifting the old wooden clock.

They shoved and pushed and heaved and towed. They bashed the corners. They somehow managed to hit the ceiling light. They banged into the other furniture and even broke a banister, but slowly and

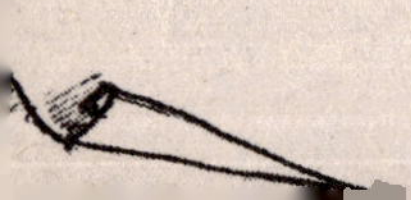

surely they eased the clock downward. They slipped and slid as they went. They trapped their fingers and hit their heads. They dropped it once or twice and it clattered and banged inside. But they kept going, until at last it was at the doorway to the dolls' house.

"Now what?" said Lily.

Button whistled.

"What was that for?"

And from a tiny hole far away in the baseboard, they came.

"Oh, ha ha. Your beetle friends. We know you've got them trained as a circus act, Button. But what use are they really?"

"You'll see." Button winked at Lily,

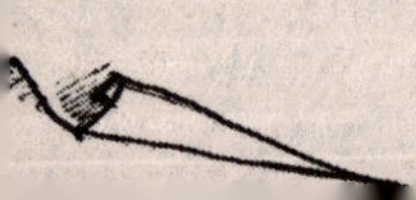

and waited. A moment later a small black beetle appeared around the corner, made a clicking sound, and more followed. Fifteen, maybe. Button stopped and counted. Twenty. They lined up side by side, head to tail, until they were organized into a long block of armored arms and legs.

Each time they were all in place one would start to stray and Button would grab hold of it and drag it back by its shell. And then one would be facing the wrong way or get distracted and it was a little bit like herding cats but, eventually, they seemed to understand.

“Good,” Button said.

Lily chuckled as she watched him. "Do you REALLY think they understand you, Button?"

"OK," he said, ignoring her. "Let's lower her down. Steady away." And they gently eased the clock onto the backs of

the small beetle army until it had 120 legs beneath it.

"Quick march!" said Button, and the clock walked itself slowly across the shop floor.

Click click click. Button knew they might have to fend off the mice. There was nothing they liked more than a quick beetle snack. But he hoped that since the mice were munching marshmallow and cheese, his little friends would be in the clear.

Lily looked anxiously down the hallway corridor. She knew Mr. Tooey must be close to finishing his lunch.

They click-click-clicked across the tiles. Button and Lily darted between the

odds and ends, keeping a close lookout for anything that might stop the beetles in their tracks. Sometimes they needed steering. Button held the back end of the clock and pushed it in the right direction, and once or twice they bumped into a table

leg or a box and the bug squadron needed putting back together again.

Lily heard movement from the kitchen. The clatter of things being put away. Cupboards closing and plates clattering.

"He's coming!"

"Nearly there," smiled Button, but Lily could see the nervousness on his face.

They stopped short next to the old bottle. A moustached face poked out of the bottle neck.

"I say, old chap, what the devil have you got there?" exclaimed the Captain.

"Throw me a line!" requested Button.

And shortly an old length of shoelace came rolling down toward them, while

Old Uncle Noggin secured it to the mast.

The beetles scattered and Button gave a salute to thank them, as Lily tied the rope tightly around the clock.

Up it went. It swung and tilted this way and that, occasionally looking like it might crash to the ground. But in the end it somehow wound its way up to the neck and was hauled on board by the curious Captain and Uncle Noggin.

Lily and Button needed the shoelace back to climb up to the bottle. And just as they waited for their shipmates to untie the clock and save them from being stranded, Mr. Tooey came walking down the corridor.

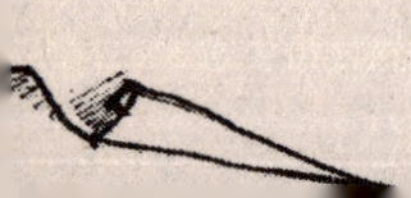

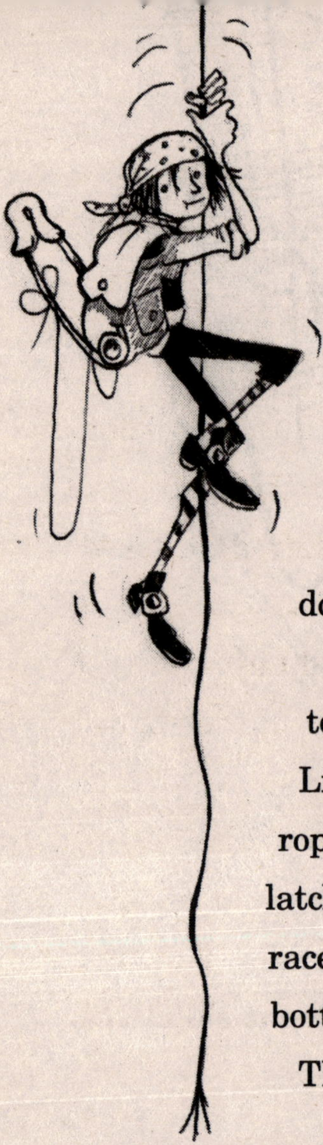

"Hurry up, Uncle Noggin," shouted Button. "Old Tooey's here!"

At last the shoelace came rolling back down at them.

"You first," said Button, trying not to panic. Lily pulled her way up the rope like a monkey. Button latched on behind her and raced up to the neck of the bottle.

They pulled the rope in

behind them. They were home.

“Fingers crossed we’re going back on the shelf!” said Lily.

“I do hope so,” said Button, sitting down at the little round porthole.

“All crew ready for takeoff?” asked the Captain.

“Fasten seat belts,” said Lily.

“Shortly ascending to a height of approximately five feet,” said Uncle Noggin.

Button looked out. He could see the pattern of Mr. Tooey’s paisley pajamas against the window. He felt the ship wobble and lift. He closed his eyes.

It was a short journey.

"All crew ready for landing," announced the Captain.

"I feel seasick," groaned Button.

"Nearly there," said Lily. She reached across and touched his arm, and he smiled back at her.

"Weird day, Lil."

"Yeah, I know. Different, eh?"

Then they felt a jolt, and they knew they were back where they belonged.

The Clock Mender

"There you go," said Button, wiping his brow with a corner of his shirt and standing back to admire the grandfather clock. Lily took off her hat and did the same.

"What a beauty. Who needs gold?" said Old Uncle Noggin.

"It's still not right," said Captain

Crabsticks. "We haven't got any pirate gold and a pirate ship isn't a pirate ship without pirate gold."

And he turned his back on the old clock.

"Oh come on, Cap'n," said Button. "She's a beauty. Look at that face. Look at that hand carving. 'Tis a work of art, sir."

"Hmmm. Well, I'll bet my moustache the old blighter doesn't even work."

"Oh well, so much for him being grateful," said Lily, folding her arms and sending an angry glare toward the Captain.

"Of course she'll work. Just needs cranking up," said Button. "I bet she'll keep good time when she's up and running."

"Well, we'll see about that." And the

Captain wandered off to ponder by himself on the tidy shelf.

Button took the crank from the back of the clock and placed it on the shaft. It fit neatly. He turned it slowly, working out the right direction, then kneeled down, taking a stronger hold. For a moment it moved, giving a satisfying *click*, *click*, *click*, but then it stuck, as if the workings were jammed. Almost as if they had decided enough was enough and they weren't going to tell the time anymore.

Button was worried about forcing it. He knew the workings of a clock were delicate—he'd seen the wristwatch in a thousand pieces, and he'd spent time in

an old cuckoo clock before someone had bought it from the junk shop.

"I'd better open the case and look inside," sighed Button.

"Do you know what you're doing?" asked Lily.

"No, not really," he replied. "Does anyone else?"

"Don't ask me!" said Old Uncle Noggin. "Steer clear of timepieces, I do. Once, a long time ago, I got stuck inside a wall clock. Couldn't escape. Only managed to get out when I'd lost weight and managed to squeeze out through a hole in the back. Took me nearly a week, it did. Never been so hungry in all my life."

“I need my tools,” said Button, who wasn’t really listening to Uncle Noggin’s tale. He headed off and came back quickly with a bent nail and half a broken paper clip.

“What’s your plan?” asked Lily.

“I think I need to get inside the back of the clock,” said Button. “The paper clip is to pick the lock with.”

“And your crowbar?”

He smiled. “In case the clip doesn’t work.”

Lily could see the determination on Button’s face. She knew she had to let him get on with it.

For what seemed like ages, Button

turned the paper clip inside the lock. This way and that, up and down, in and out.

The Captain had wandered back. "I say, old chap, still tinkering with that old contraption? I'll be hungry soon. Time to divert to the kitchen, I think."

Lily knew that if there was one thing about Button it was that he never gave in.

Suddenly the door sprang open. It had worked! But what Button found inside was not at all what he expected.

A smile broke across his face.

"What is it?" asked Lily. "Why are you grinning like that?"

"You'll never guess what's jamming up the workings," laughed Button.

"Ahh, don't tell me," said Old Uncle Noggin. "Is it pie? I love a good pie."

"You see, I knew there'd be something wrong," muttered the Captain, wandering back in. "I knew it wouldn't work."

"Huh, maybe we broke the workings when we moved it," said Lily. "Is it broken cogs and wheels?"

"No it's not. Not at all," said Button. "It's this . . ."

And with both hands he pulled out a long shining gold chain that had been tucked into the case.

"At last," Button said, "we have our pirate gold! Still disappointed with your grandfather clock, Captain?"

"My my my, what a marvelous find, Button, you old treasure," exclaimed the Captain. "I knew that clock was good luck as soon as I saw it. Didn't I say so? Didn't I say so?"

Lily rolled her eyes and folded her arms.

"Hee hee, you've struck gold, lad," said Old Uncle Noggin. "You see, Cap'n! It's just like my story about the astronomer. You were so busy looking elsewhere, you didn't realize what was there in front of you."

"Ha, I suppose so," chuckled Captain Crabsticks.

Button held the long chain in his hands. Big chunky links of glimmering gold.

"No wonder that clock was so difficult to maneuver!" complained Lily. "That's why my back feels stiff and my hands still hurt."

"It was worth the pain," said Button, forgetting his bruises.

They stood and stared at the gold. The shining yellow caught the light, gleaming back at them and coloring their faces.

In the middle of the chain was a locket held together with a clasp. It was oval-shaped, brimming with swirls and wisps of leaf pattern. Button pulled on the clasp with both hands. Inside was a tiny diamond! It caught the light and shimmered back at him.

Button was so astonished he dropped to his knees with the twinkling treasure still in his hands. "Look at that!"

"Treasures beyond what we could ever have expected," said the Captain, his eyes and mouth wide open.

"And maybe now we can get your clock working," said Lily.

Button rested the chain on the floor and went back to work. He closed the casing on the clock and turned the crank until the shaft clicked satisfyingly for several rotations . . . then suddenly the clock came to life.

Ticktock—ticktock—ticktock.

They could hear cars out on the road

heading home and Button knew it was coming up to five o'clock. He turned the hands into position, took a step back, and smiled a long smile. It had been worth it.

"That's the clock working," he said. "Time to put the rest of our home back together."

King Midas

It was always good to get to the evening and reflect on the adventures of the day. And what a day it had been. Captain Crabsticks was asleep and the rest of them were sitting around the lighted candle, ready for one of Old Uncle Noggin's stories.

The ship was back in order, and looking spick-and-span.

"What was your best bit of today?" Lily asked Button.

"I'm not sure," said Button. "Maybe it was the earwig battle. Or maybe it was finding gold in the clock. I can't decide."

"Definitely the diamond for me!" said Lily. "I wasn't too keen on the earwigs. They tore my stripy pirate leggings."

"Huh, well, there's no competition if you ask me," mumbled Old Uncle Noggin. They could barely make out the words, his mouth was so full.

“What on earth is he eating?” asked Lily.

“Oh, Mr. Tooey left a bit of pasty on the shelf,” explained Button. “Cheese and onion too! We should have enough for the next couple of days as long as we can keep it hidden. And as long as he doesn’t scoff the lot of it.”

“BRILLIANT,” said Lily. “My favorite. Cheese and pastry is the best thing on earth.”

“Mr. Tooey’s a strange man. How could ANYONE forget they had a cheese-and-onion pasty? You can keep your treasure,” said Old Uncle Noggin. “This is what I call pirate gold.”

“I thought he’d already eaten,” said Lily.

“That was his evening meal,” said Button.

“So what’s this?” Lily asked.

“Supper!”

Lily and Button chuckled together as they carried on with their task. They were unpicking all the knots and tangles from the gold chain and laying it out along the shelf.

“Don’t you gct yourselves too concerned with gold and riches,” said Old Uncle Noggin, settling back on a piece of sponge.

“What do you mean?” asked Button.

“It be dangerous, Button. Greed for gold leads to trouble. You’re far better off concentrating on the food cupboard than the treasure chest.”

"How can it be dangerous?" said Lily, staring at the gold as it shimmered magically in the candlelight.

"Let me tell you a story," said Uncle Noggin. "A story that'll explain it better than I can."

He lay back on his dish sponge, licking the last bits of food from his fingers and

wiping his hands on the purple underpants blanket.

"Once there was a king called Midas. He was a good man, but foolish, and his desire for riches was the end of him.

"He loved gold, you see. He loved it so much that when the god Dionysus offered to grant him a wish, he asked that everything he touched should turn to gold. That way, he knew he would be happy.

"But this was far from the truth."

"Why?" asked Button. "If everything you touched turned to gold, you would be rich for the rest of your life."

"You are right," said Old Uncle Noggin with a smile. "At first he was delighted and went around practicing his new skill. He touched the walls. They turned to gold. He touched the trees outside. They turned to gold.

"After a while he became thirsty. But as soon as the wine touched his lips, it turned to gold. When he put food to his mouth, the same thing happened. And so the very thing he had desired became the end of him. King Midas was no more.

"So be careful, my little gold-diggers. Greed is your enemy." And Old Uncle Noggin lay back in his sponge and closed his eyes.

"He wasn't saying that when he was stuffing his face with pastry," pointed out Lily.

"I heard that," muttered Old Uncle Noggin. But in an instant he was asleep, snoring so hard that his breath blew the candle flame this way and that.

Everyone except Button and Lily was asleep. Even Jones.

It was dark, except for the glow of the candle and the orange of the street lamp. A slight chill found them and they pulled their little blankets around themselves.

"Do you ever get scared?" asked Lily.

"Scared of what?"

"I don't know. Anything. Everything. Out here at night, all on our own. Where anything could happen."

"What's brought this on?" asked Button.

"I don't know. I just got to thinking that . . . well, now we've got riches on board, maybe . . ." She stopped.

"Maybe WHAT, Lily?"

"Maybe someone or SOMETHING might come and steal our treasure. You know, in the night . . . Do you think we're safe?"

Button got to his feet. He walked to the edge of the shelf and gazed across the familiar shapes of the shop.

"We're safe," he assured her. "For now, anyway."

They snuffed out the candlelight and wrapped up warm. Jones woke for a moment and came and tucked his head into Button's middle.

"Goodnight, Lily," said Button. "See you in the morning."

"Goodnight," said Lily. "Maybe we can have a quiet day tomorrow."

"Maybe," said Button . . . "Maybe."

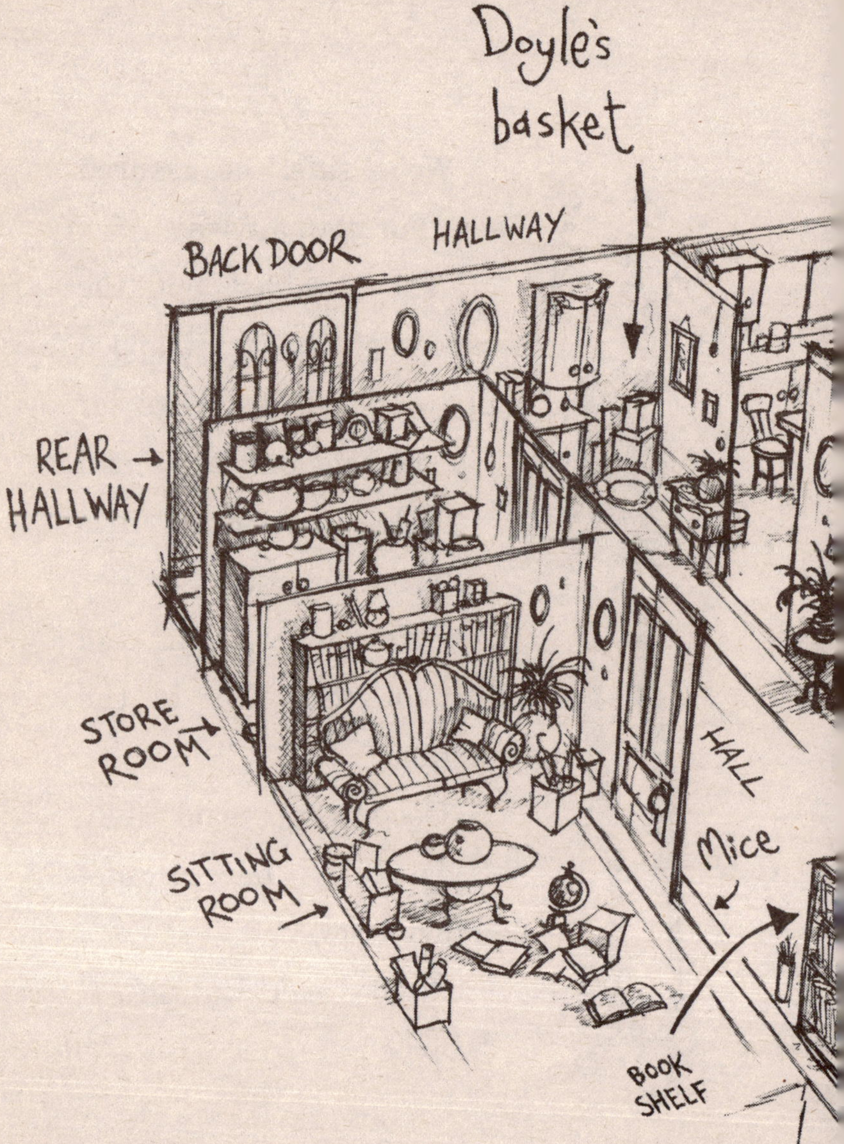

Doyle's basket
HALLWAY
BACK DOOR
REAR HALLWAY
STORE ROOM
SITTING ROOM
HALL
Mice
BOOK SHELF

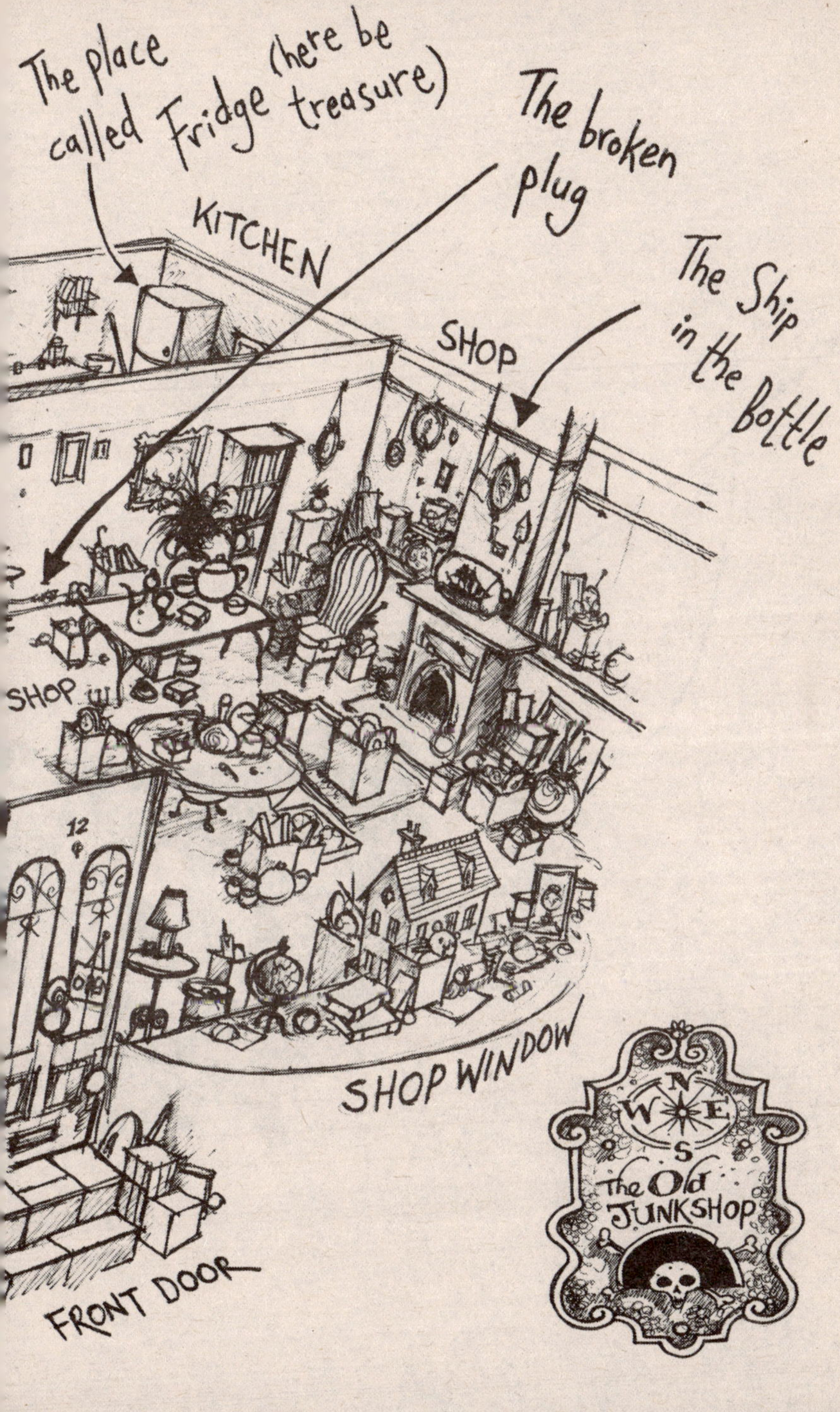

The place called Fridge (here be treasure)
The broken plug
KITCHEN
The Ship in the Bottle
SHOP
SHOP
12
SHOP WINDOW
N
W
E
S
The Old JUNKSHOP
FRONT DOOR

Turn the page for a peek at where
the Pocket Pirates adventures started:

THE GREAT CHEESE ROBBERY

Button the ship's boy had spent most of the afternoon exploring. He'd climbed in and out of piles of books and boxes of this and that to see what he might find. He'd even snatched a quick nap inside the old cuckoo clock.

But on his way back down to the shelf, Button had caught the back of his jacket on an old picture hook and now he was hanging helplessly on the wall.

"Oh, crumbs, not again," he said out loud to himself.

He looked over the shop. It was one of those perfect evenings. The moonlight was pouring in through the window and shone a silvery blue over the ship in the bottle. Everything had been calm until now. He tried to shake himself free, but it was no good.

High above Button, something had awakened in the dark. Mr. Dregby, the house spider, was keen to make a snack out of Button. He'd had his six eyes on the boy for some time. And now he could see that his perfect meal was hanging there beneath him, waiting.

"The young ones are the juiciest," Mr. Dregby cackled in delight.

Button heard a scritching sound above and he looked up in alarm. A tangle of long hairy legs and beady eyes was rushing toward him.

And then, all at once, he felt himself being pulled by the legs. He slipped clean out of his jacket and landed in a heap on

the floor, on top of his rescuer. She let out a muffled "YELP."

It was his best friend, Lily, the youngest of the pirate crew. She jumped to her feet, waving a long darning needle in Mr. Dregby's direction. The spider scuttled grumpily back into the darkness above the shelf.

"Thanks!" said Button as he straightened himself out. "That was close."

He looked up to see his coat was still hanging on the hook.

"You're not supposed to go wandering off on your own," Lily said. "It's dangerous!'

"I was looking for an adventure," Button replied.

"You shouldn't wish too hard for an adventure," said Lily. "You just might get one. . . ."

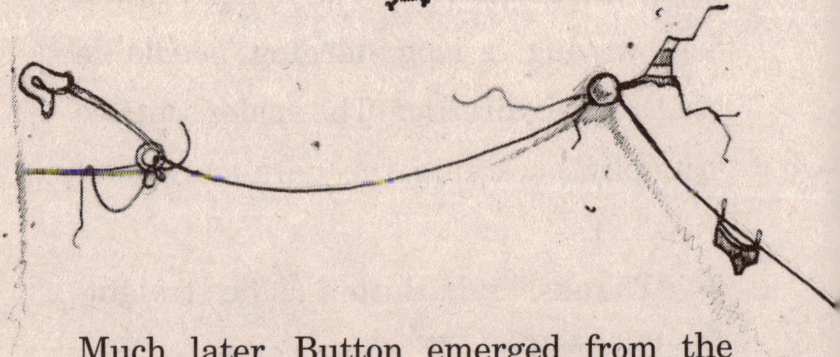

Much later, Button emerged from the ship, feeling calmer. He climbed out of the bottle's glass neck and dropped down on to the shelf.

He took a good look around the shop. All was quiet again. From his pocket, Button pulled out a pirate flag, which he unfolded and tied between a candlestick and a pin in the wall.

"Captain's orders," Button explained to a nearby beetle. "It's my job to fly the skull and crossbones, and keep this shelf polished and scrubbed as properly as the deck of the ship."

Pepper Jack, the leader of the mangy gang of mice who lived behind the junk shop baseboard, was watching Button

from a distance, his mouse ears pricked. He nodded to Blue Vinny and Fleabag, two of his gang, as they waited in the darkness. Their mean eyes shone back at him through the black.

But Button couldn't see the mice. Instead he took a seat on a small cotton reel and kicked off his buckled shoes. Jones, the ship's cat, was curled up nearby, in a peaceful snooze. Lily was warming her hands at

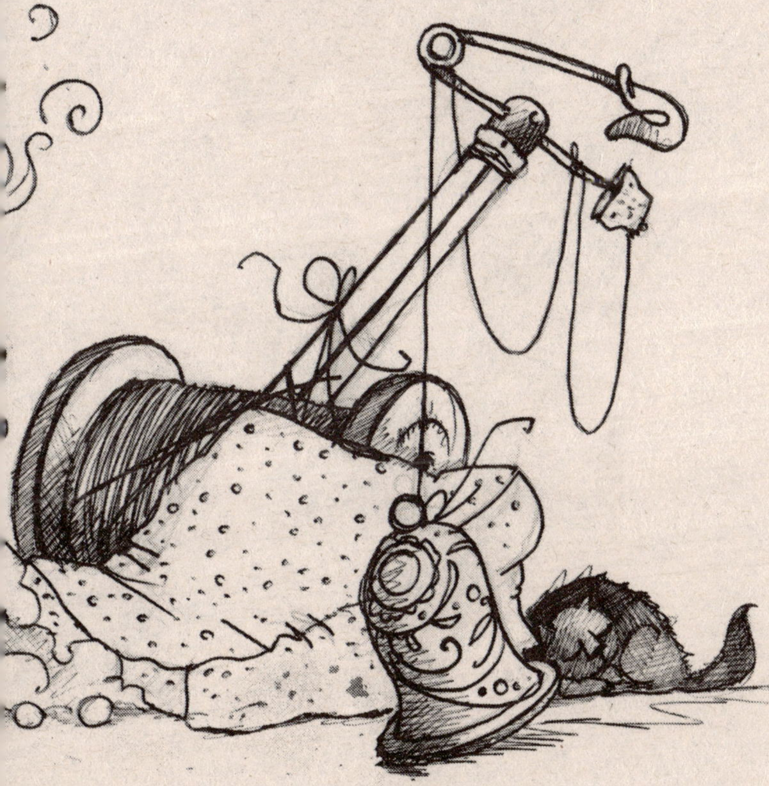

the stub of a lighted candle and quietly singing a sea shanty to herself.

The captain of the ship, Captain

Crabsticks, was having a rest on an open page of his favorite book, *Treasure Island*. He was tired after a day on the hallway shelf reading *Domestic Pest Control* and *The Pocket Encyclopedia of Trees*, which wasn't pocket-sized at all. Especially not when you are two inches high.

"Arrr, there you are, me hearties," said Old Uncle Noggin as he hobbled along to join his shipmates. He took a sip from a steaming bottle cap of hot chocolate and pulled his blanket over his knees. He was sitting

on his favorite seat, a dish sponge. "Are you ready for a good old pirate story?"

"Of course we are!" cheered Lily. She and Button loved Old Uncle Noggin's pirate tales, even though they weren't quite sure they were true.

"Is it made up?" Button asked. He was still undecided about the story of the cockroach who ate Captain Crabsticks's parrot, and the one about the pirate who sailed to the land of "next door" in a margarine tub . . . It was always hard to tell.

"Never you mind, young Button," muttered Old Uncle Noggin. "Tonight I'm telling you the story of Blackbeard's ghost, and how he went searching for his missing head and found it bobbing around in the water like an empty barrel, glowing in the dark."

All eyes and ears were fixed on Uncle Noggin. The crew were so taken with the terrifying story of Blackbeard and his ghost, they weren't aware of a very real terror that lurked nearby.

They didn't hear sharp claws scratching their way up to the shelf, or the *whoosh* of tails whipping through the air.

They didn't see the sharp teeth and long twitching snouts that cast spiky shadows across the candlelit walls.

And that was *exactly* what the baseboard mice wanted!